RABUNZEL

For my daughter, Autumn, aka Lorelei – GPJ

For Luka and Luci xx – LS

EGMONT

First published in Great Britain in 2021 by
Egmont Books UK, an imprint of HarperCollins*Publishers*
1 London Bridge Street, London SE1 9GF
www.egmontbooks.co.uk

HarperCollins*Publishers*
1st Floor, Watermarque Building, Ringsend Road, Dublin 4, Ireland

Text copyright © Gareth P. Jones 2021
Illustrations copyright © Loretta Schauer 2021

The moral rights of the author and illustrator have been asserted.

ISBN 978 1 4052 9858 2

71032/001

Printed in Italy

A CIP catalogue record for this book is available from the British Library.

RABUNZEL

Gareth P. Jones
and Loretta Schauer

EGMONT

Once up on Furry Tail Hill, in a field between a babbling blue stream and a deep, dark forest, lived a rabbit called Rabunzel.

She had a teeny, tufty tail, a tiny, twitchy nose and two wide eyes.

She also had **VERY** long ears.

So long that they trailed behind her everywhere she went . . .

creating all kinds of problems. This made Rabunzel's mother worry. Like all the animals on Furry Tail Hill, she lived in fear of the hungry-eyed creatures that lurked in the deep, dark forest.

With Rabunzel's long ears causing her so much danger, her mother decided she had to put her daughter somewhere safe, far away from the hungry-eyed creatures:

"We must keep you up high,
    you'll be safe in the sky.
    Out of harm's way,
    that's where you must stay."

KEEP OUT!

There was no way up
and no way down.
Finally, Rabunzel
was safe and sound.
And all alone.

Each morning, Rabunzel's mother
arrived with a basket of carrots,
lettuce and fresh water.

"Rabunzel, Rabunzel, let down your ears!"
she would call out.

"Just a minute," Rabunzel
would respond.

Then she'd unfurl her long
ears and allow her mother
to climb up.

Rabunzel would gaze at her friends running, jumping and laughing in the field below. How she longed to play with them again!

She begged her mother to let her come down, but the reply was always the same:

"We must keep you up high, you're safe in the sky. Out of harm's way, that's where you must stay."

For many **DAYS,**
WEEKS,
MONTHS,
Rabunzel remained
up high, safe
and sound . . .

and **BORED TO BITS,** with nothing to do
except brush her long ears and try to keep fit.

Then one day, a hare called Flash Harry came racing into the field up on Furry Tail Hill. He heard Rabunzel's mother call,

"Rabunzel, Rabunzel, let down your ears!"

KEEP OUT!

DO NOT CLIMB

Flash Harry had never seen anything like it . . . nor anyone as beautiful as Rabunzel.

"Such beauty should not be hidden away," he proclaimed. "I, Flash Harry the Hare, will rescue her."

The next day, Flash Harry called in a high-pitched voice,

"Rabunzel, Rabunzel, let down your ears!"

Assuming it was her mother, Rabunzel lobbed down her lobes.

Flash Harry heaved and huffed as he climbed his way up.

But when Rabunzel saw that he was not her mother . . .

KER-SPLANG!

"I didn't mean to alarm you," said Flash Harry. "I'm here to rescue you."

"That's very kind of you," began Rabunzel, "but I . . ."

However, Flash Harry wasn't listening. He grabbed Rabunzel and . . .

jumped!

Together, rabbit and hare drifted down to the ground, Rabunzel's ears fluttering behind them like ribbons.

As Rabunzel was gathering up her ears,
her mother hopped out and cried,
"What are you doing down here?"

**"Fear not. She is under
my protection now,"**
replied Flash Harry.

"You?" said Rabunzel's mother.
**"You are a stranger, and your
reckless behaviour has placed
her in danger."**

But she wasn't the only one to have noticed that Rabunzel was no longer hidden away. The hungry-eyed creatures drew near.

"Quick, I will carry you to safety!" urged Flash Harry. "I won't let you down."

"You must let down this hare," ordered Rabunzel's mother, "and return to your tree at once."

While her mother and Flash Harry bickered, Rabunzel kept her eyes trained on the hungry-eyed creatures approaching. Then she . . .

. . . spun around, sending her ears soaring through the air and slicing the long grass.

With perfect poise and exquisite aim, she swung her ears once . . . twice . . . then again.

She **WRAPPED** them

and **FLAPPED** them,

WHIPPED them

and **SNAPPED** them.

POW!

The hungry-eyed creatures
had met their match.
They turned and fled.
They never looked back.

Every animal up on Furry Tail Hill stared at Rabunzel
in wonder. Rabunzel turned to her mother and smiled:

"My ears may be long,
   but they're nimble and strong.
I won't hide in fear,
   I'll live proudly down here."

Then she said to Flash Harry:

"You offered to save me
   from my mother's high hutch.
I don't really need saving,
   though, thanks very much."

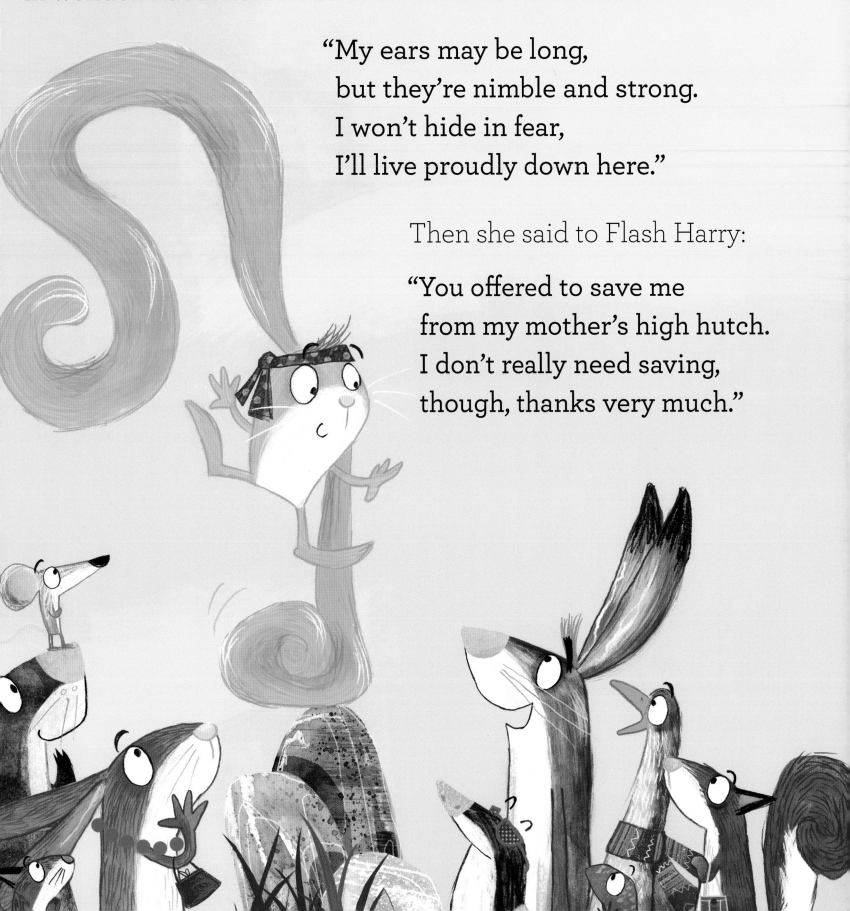

From that day onwards, whenever there was trouble, the cry would go up,

"Rabunzel, Rabunzel, let down your ears!"

Then she would send
the hungry-eyed
creatures running.

And up on Furry Tail Hill,
Rabunzel and her friends lived
happily, hoppily and safely ever after.

LOOK OUT FOR THE NEXT FAIRY TALE FOR THE FEARLESS IN AUTUMN 2021!